The Magical Love Box

Written by Mary Reinhart
Illustrated by Shawn McCann

Published in the USA by Milsará, LLC, Milwaukee, WI
Gift Edition (8" x 10") ISBN: 978-1-7327893-1-9

Also available on Amazon ISBN: 978-1-7327893-1-9
and from Ingram ISBN: 978-1-7327893-0-2

Printed in the USA by Worzalla, Stevens Point, WI

Library of Congress Control Number: 2018908452

For bulk purchases, gift orders of the signed book, or to set up visits of author and/or illustrator to your classroom or organization, or for curriculum ideas, visit:
www.maryreinhartbooks.com or email Mary at **maryreinhartbooks@gmail.com**

Interior design by Robin Krauss
www.bookformatters.com

Cover and interior illustrations by Shawn McCann
www.shawnmccann.com
The illustrations for this book were done in acrylic on collaged paper.

The Magical Love Box

A Book for All Ages

Milsará

Milsará, LLC
401 E Beaumont Ave Suite 414
Milwaukee, WI 53217

This is a book where love is shared through

The Magic of a Box

It's a story about giving and receiving.

It's a story about magic!

It's a story about love!

The Magical Love Box, with its abundance of shapes, colors, and objects, is sure to appeal to the child's own world. The message at its heart—love's power to connect—is wrapped in a whimsical exercise in problem solving. Destined to become a frequently requested bedtime book.

Brian F. Doherty, Ph.D, University of Texas, Dept. of Literature

The Magical Love Box brings to life the special connection between grandparents and grandchildren—a bond of focused attention, wonder, shared inquiry, laughter and fun, trust, and unconditional love. It is a book for children and adults to read and enjoy together as they savor their own Magical Love Box relationships.

Judy F. Carr, Ed.D., Education Consultant, Center for Curriculum Renewal LLC

As an adult reader, I was moved by *The Magical Love Box*. The story anchors the reader in the universal truth of love. Through Jack's journey, he discovers that, by persevering, a solution will be revealed. His discovery is magical: as he gives his love, love rains back on him. This book drew me into my inner child.

Valerie Kratz, CEO, HVS Labs, Inc.

The Magical Love Box will certainly enhance your classroom. The great problem solving that the main character experiences will be a jumping off point to guide students to engage in sound problem-solving skills. The beautiful writing and illustrations will keep your students engaged from beginning to end. It's a must for every classroom.

Jane Elizabeth Marko, MS

I'm always looking for a powerful book to share with my grandchildren and this is it. *The Magical Love Box* completely engaged my grandkids and sparked heartfelt conversation about love and family. My grandkids regularly place *The Magical Love Box* in the Grandma-will-read-to-us pile. I'm as excited to read it as they are to hear it read.

Grandma Bessy

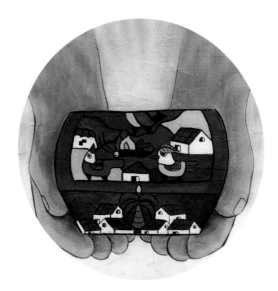

To my children and grandchildren
and to all beings everywhere
that we may all know the
magic of love.

On a sunny day in April, a small package arrived at Jack's house. It was a birthday present for Jack from Kamama, his grandma.

Jack was very excited.
He liked getting presents.

What could be inside the package? he wondered. He could hardly wait for Daddy to come home so the family could celebrate his birthday together.

Mommy fixed pizza, his favorite dinner, and after everyone had finished eating, it was finally time for Jack to open his present.

Jack's little
brother, James,
helped tug on the ribbon, and
they both tore off the wrapping paper.
At last the package was open.

There, in front of him, was the most colorful box Jack had ever seen. The design on the small, wooden box had been carefully painted by native people of El Salvador, a country in Central America, far, far away from where Jack lived.

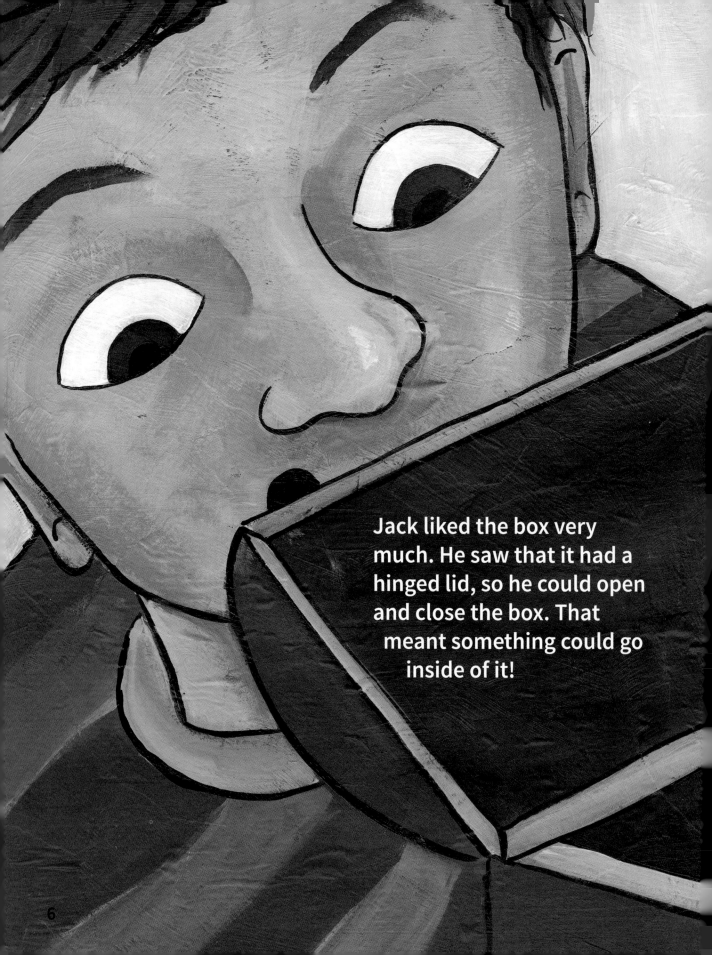

Jack liked the box very much. He saw that it had a hinged lid, so he could open and close the box. That meant something could go inside of it!

"It will have to be just the right thing because this is a very special box," he said to himself.

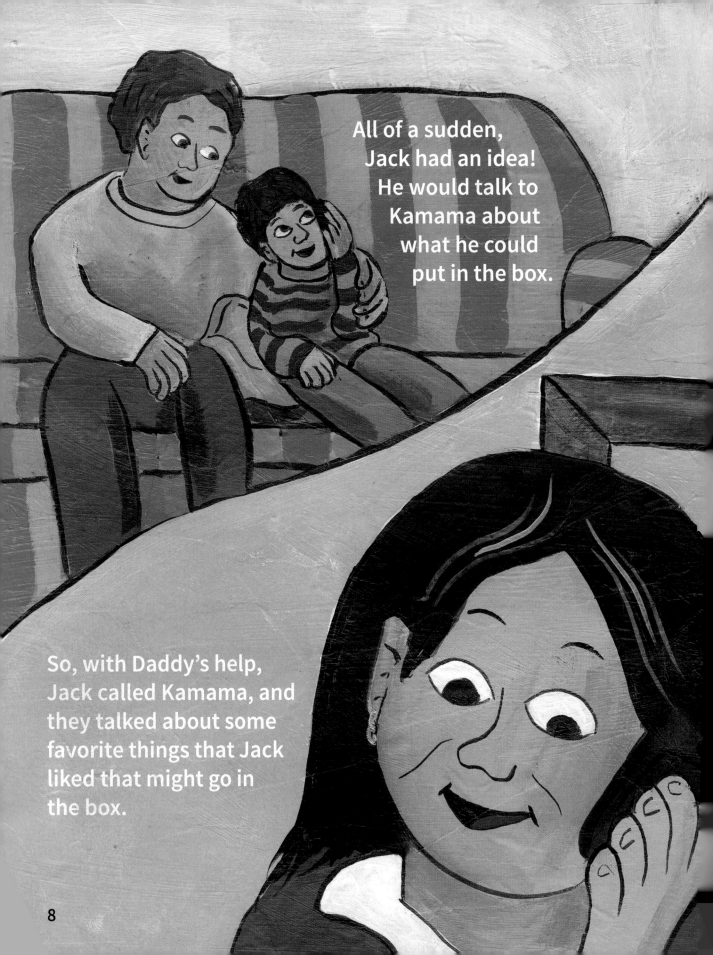

All of a sudden, Jack had an idea! He would talk to Kamama about what he could put in the box.

So, with Daddy's help, Jack called Kamama, and they talked about some favorite things that Jack liked that might go in the box.

"I know!" said Jack. "I will put the tractor I made out of building blocks in my special box."

"How is that possible?" asked Kamama.

Hmmmmm . . .

"Oh no, that isn't possible," Jack said. "The tractor is too big."

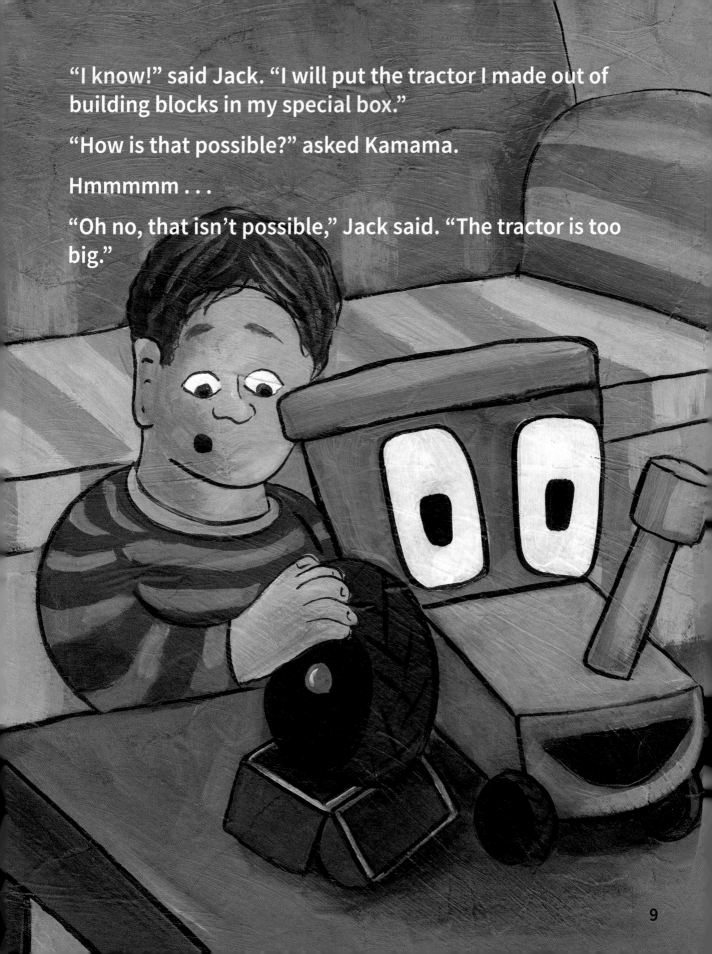

"I know!" said Jack. "I will put one of my favorite stuffed animals, the giraffe, in my special box."

"How is that possible?" asked Kamama.

Hmmmmm . . .

"Oh no, that isn't possible," said Jack. "The giraffe is too tall."

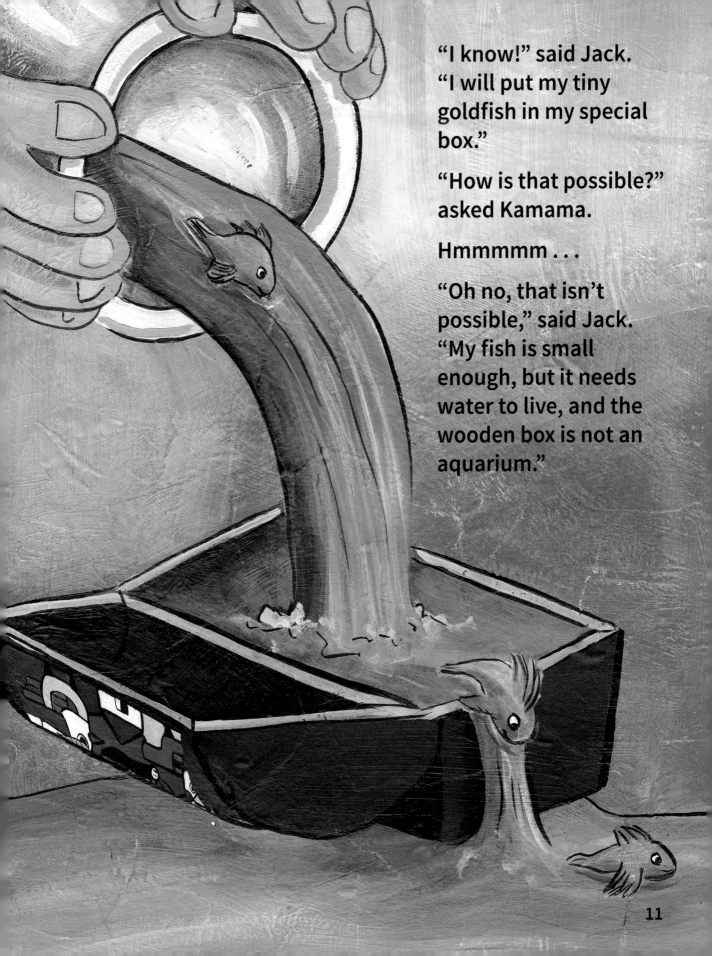

"I know!" said Jack. "I will put my tiny goldfish in my special box."

"How is that possible?" asked Kamama.

Hmmmmm . . .

"Oh no, that isn't possible," said Jack. "My fish is small enough, but it needs water to live, and the wooden box is not an aquarium."

Jack was stuck! He tried and tried to think of just the right thing to put in the box, but nothing he thought of seemed to work. He shook the box. He held it to his ear.

He looked inside it again as he tried to figure out what he most wanted to put inside his box.

Kamama told him not to worry—that sometimes it helps to just let it be, and sooner or later, the answer will come.

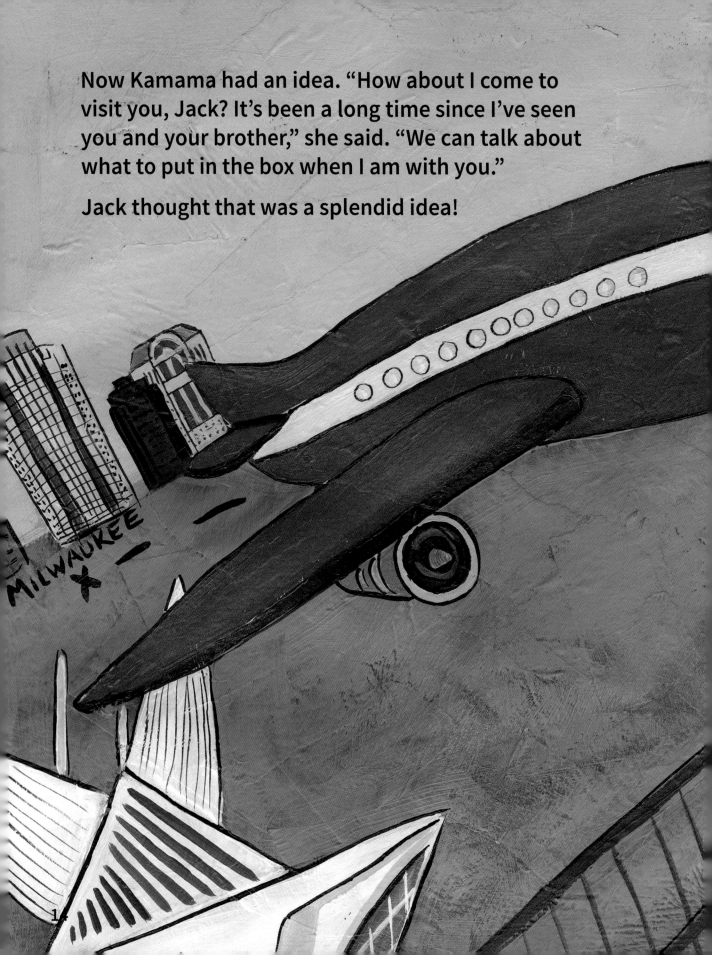

Now Kamama had an idea. "How about I come to visit you, Jack? It's been a long time since I've seen you and your brother," she said. "We can talk about what to put in the box when I am with you."

Jack thought that was a splendid idea!

MILWAUKEE
X

So the next day, Kamama went to the airport to get on a red and yellow airplane. She was very excited to see her grandchildren!

SAN FRANCISCO

15

It was late in the afternoon when Kamama arrived at Jack's house. The two brothers had just finished their dinner.

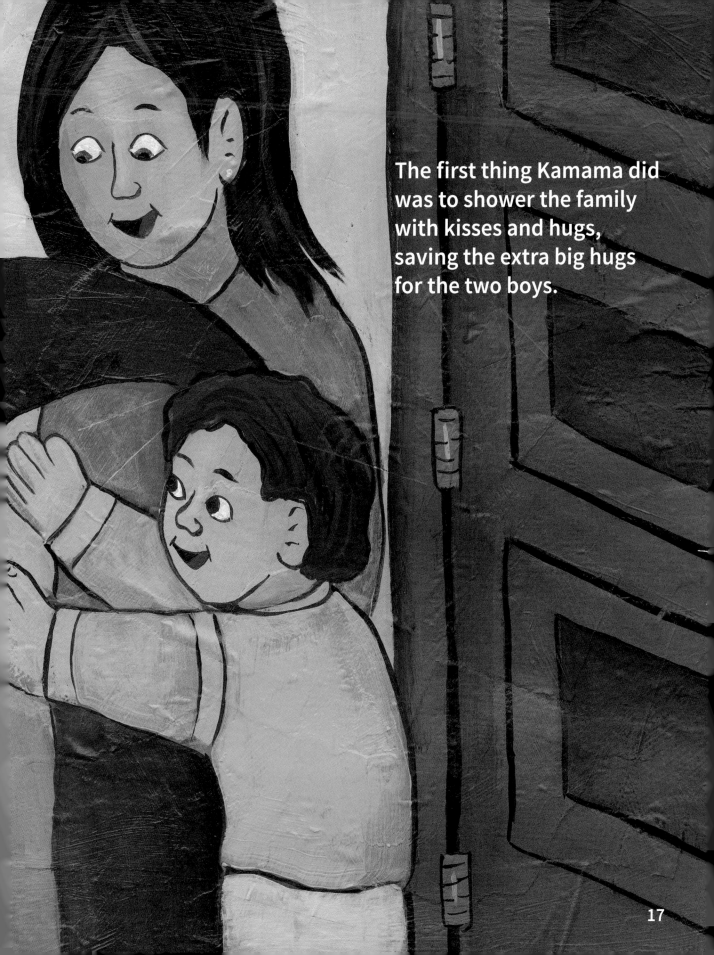

The first thing Kamama did was to shower the family with kisses and hugs, saving the extra big hugs for the two boys.

Daddy took James upstairs for his bath while Mommy cleaned up the kitchen after fixing a very good dinner for her family.

Jack led Kamama by the hand into the living room. He wanted Kamama to read him some books before going up to his bedroom, where he kept the special box.

They sat down on the striped sofa. Jack looked around the room; then he looked up at Kamama, and said "I love it here."

"Do you mean in this house?" asked Kamama.

"Yes, it's a very nice house," said Jack.

Kamama smiled and said that it was indeed a very nice house for two wonderful little boys.

"I wish I could put the house in my special box," said Jack with a smile. "But I know that isn't possible!" They both giggled at the thought.

They read two of Jack's favorite books together, and then it was time for Jack to get ready for bed.

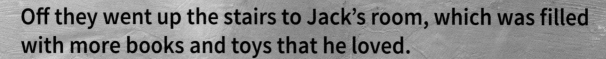

Off they went up the stairs to Jack's room, which was filled with more books and toys that he loved.

Before they talked about the special box, Kamama asked Jack to show her how grown up he was by getting himself ready for bed.

So, after he took off his green shirt, his khaki pants, and his blue socks, Kamama asked him to put them in the hamper.

Jack looked at Kamama quizzically and said, "Oh, Kamama, you're so silly! That's not a hamper; that's a laundry basket."

And they both had a good laugh together.

After Jack put on his rocket pajamas and brushed his teeth, Kamama asked Jack to get the special box from his bookshelf.

"Oh, finally!" Jack thought. He had been so patient, waiting to talk about what to put in the box.

After all, he knew he couldn't put his tractor in the box. That wasn't possible. It was too big.

He couldn't put his giraffe in the box. That wasn't possible. It was too tall.

He couldn't put his fish in the box. That wasn't possible. It needed water.

And he surely couldn't put his house that he loved in the box.

Jack looked up at his grandma as they sat on the bean bag chair and said, "Kamama, I thought about putting you in the box so I could have you near me all the time, but now I know that's not possible either."

"Well, Jack, you could put my hugs in the box if you want," said Kamama.

Hmmmm . . .

Jack thought about that for a while. "Wait, Kamama. I have another idea! I want to fill my box with MY hugs for all my family. I want to name my box the Love Box. I will imagine putting all the hugs I have inside me in my special box. I will give love to all my family every night before I go to bed."

Jack was excited about his plans for the box. In his mind's eye, he saw his hugs floating among the soft clouds, going out to Mommy and Daddy, his brother, his grandmas and his grandpas, his aunts and his uncles, his cousins, and his friends . . . and Shelby, his dog.

He put the box on his dresser next to his bed and fell asleep.

But hold on! Something magical happened during the stillness of the night. All the hugs that Jack put in the box for his family came right back—from them to him. Right there, in Jack's special box!

When Jack woke up the next morning, he went to his Love Box and gently opened it, peeking inside.

Oh so many hugs! From all of his family! He lifted the box carefully over his head, so that all the hugs fell all around him, wrapping his whole body in love.

Happily, he exclaimed, "This isn't just a Love Box; it's a *Magical Love Box*. And now I am loved all day long!"

Let's Talk About the Book!

1. What would you put in your box?

2. Jack was very excited when he received the box. What situations in your life make you feel happy and excited?

3. Let's talk about times when you have felt love and kindness.

4. Let's talk about times when you have shared love and kindness.

5. Think about being outside. Think about being in a mall, a church, a park. Anywhere that's not your house. Let's talk about when you have noticed kindness and love in those places.

6. Where would you keep hugs and love in your house?

7. How do you feel when someone makes you feel special?

8. How do you feel when you make someone feel special?

9. How do you think sharing love and kindness can change a person's day?

10. How do you think sharing love and kindness can change the world?

Thank You

So many people have contributed to making this magical love story a reality:

Shawn McCann, my amazing illustrator; Robin Krauss, my very skilled graphic designer; Jane Marko and Jean Wilker, my checks-and-balances; Lori Dutter, art contributor; Nancy Buchanan, Judy Carr, Kelly Condon, Brian Doherty, Susan Harris, Bev Heyer, Mike Heyer, Valerie Kratz, Susie Rozanski, and Emmy Rozanski for their invaluable insight.

It is my sincere hope that, though not mentioned here by name, you may know in your heart that I am forever grateful to all of you who have given your support, critical eye, suggestions, encouragement, kindness and friendship.

Nothing in this life is accomplished alone. It takes community.

The Author

Mary Reinhart, known to her grandchildren as "Kamama," has the gift of seeing the wonderment of the world as experienced through the eyes of the young. Her first career in teaching allowed her to celebrate life's curiosity along with her students. As a wife and mother, she explored more of the love and joys of daily living. Widowed at a young age, life's journey led her into a second career as a facilitator of alternative healing and wellness practices.

Kade'n Kian Photography

Through years of embracing the opportunity to engage in storytelling with her eleven grandchildren, Mary became inspired to put on paper the compassion, joy, and love that she and her grandchildren share.

She came to know that what matters most in life is that we give the love that is innately present in all of us and open our hearts to receive this wondrous gift of love from others.

Mary lives in Whitefish Bay, Wisconsin. Her two youngest grandchildren are the inspiration for *The Magical Love Box.*

Why do Mary's grandchildren call her "Kamama"?

While working at a wellness center in 2000, Mary asked her friend, Arrowhawk, a Cherokee Native American, the name for "grandma" in his native tongue. It is "tsala-gi." A beautiful word, but it wasn't easy to say.

So she checked out other words in the Cherokee language, starting with the letter A. When she got to the word "kamama," she liked its sound. The meaning? Butterfly! Perfect! Mary has loved butterflies ever since she was a little girl. Can you find the two hidden butterflies in the book?

The Illustrator

As an artist, **Shawn McCann** is one who loves to explore the relationship of art, space, and interaction. Having graduated from the Minneapolis College of Art and Design with a BFA, Shawn has grown into a multi-media, multi-disciplinary artist whose work explores color, texture, form, and content. Within each of these areas, each project has been created with its own voice, its own character, and culminates in a rich experience for the viewer.

As a respected illustrator of children's books, Shawn adds the spark that is needed to bring the books alive! He is currently president of the Children's Book Illustrators Guild of Minnesota, Board of Directors member at the Minnesota Center for Book Arts (MCBA), member of the Society of Children's Book Writers and Illustrators, and past vice president and member of the Minneapolis College of Art and Design Alumni Board of Directors.

Lori Voskuil-Dutter is a rural Wisconsin artist whose work has been enjoyed by people across the country for over three decades. She has earned numerous awards and ribbons at various art exhibits throughout her career. Her deep reverence for nature and its inhabitants is reflected in each piece of her art and verse.

The idea for this piece of artwork came about after Mary watched an emotional acceptance speech by Lyn-Manuel Miranda at the Tony Awards in 2016. Mr. Miranda repeatedly spoke the words 'Love Is' as hearts were filled with much needed hope for our world and our children. While writing the book, *The Magical Love Box*, Mary asked artist, Lori Dutter, to capture those words in illustration. It is an honor to include her art in the *The Magical Love Box*, as a reminder for all ages to constantly be inspired by the power of love!